Ruben and Archie

# To Be the Same or Not to Be the Same

Story : Ju-Yarn Tsai
Illustrations : Chih-Ming Huang
English Translation Team :
Yi-Hui Su and Christopher Heise

The Corporate Body of the Buddha Educational Foundation

In the big Tee-Hee Field, everyone knew Ruben the Giraffe and Archie the Little Ant were the closest pals. Archie liked to lie in the hairy groove between Ruben's short rounded horns and comfortably fall asleep.

Often, when the moon rose and lit up the field, even though Ruben started to get hungry and his tummy rumbled, he didn't want to wake Archie up.

One day, Archie woke up drooling in the soft hairy cradle on Ruben's head. He yawned, and felt lucky and grateful.

"Ruben is so nice to me. He brought me to this height so I could see the world. In return, I'll invite him to my house!"

Ruben accepted the invitation, since he also wanted to see Archie's underground world. How different would it be, compared to his, looking down from the clouds?

"Where is it?"
"Is it here?"
"Or there?"

"It's over here!"

Ruben lowered his head to
the ground with his eyes
wide open.
"Wow, it's so tiny!"

Ruben was surprised, “I can only see it when I get close!”
"Welcome!"
“It’s really narrow!”

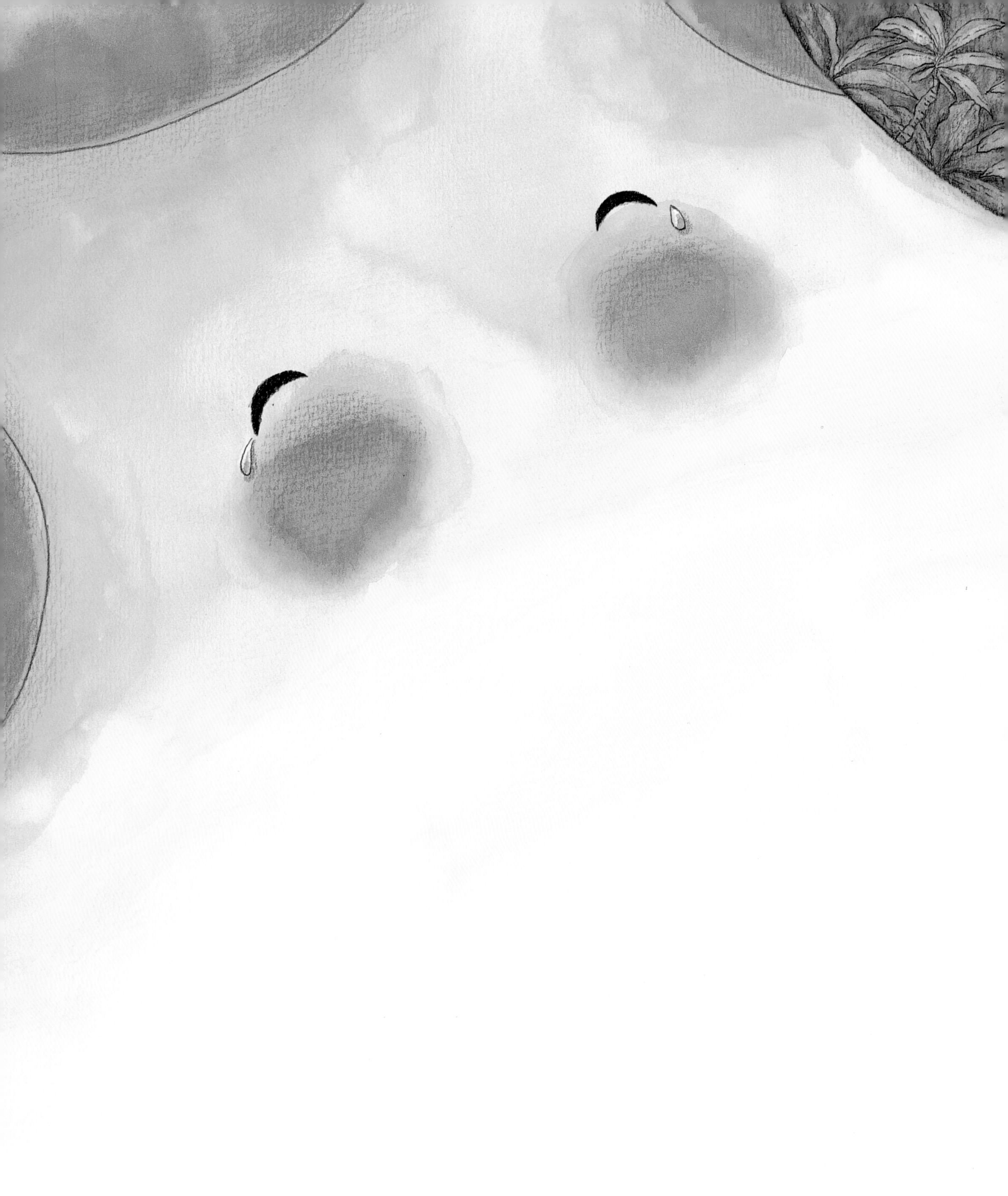

Archie was sitting among his toys and holding his favorite stuffed giraffe in his arms. He said contently, “I love my home so much.”

"These are my treasures."

Ruben replied with a smile, “Well, first of all, it would have to be extremely high!”

Archie could not help asking, "Ruben, how would you decorate your own home if you had one?"

Ruben decided to stay
overnight at Archie's place, and
they talked about how to build
a house for giraffes.
That night, Archie had a dream
where he and Ruben built many
houses in different
shapes and sizes.

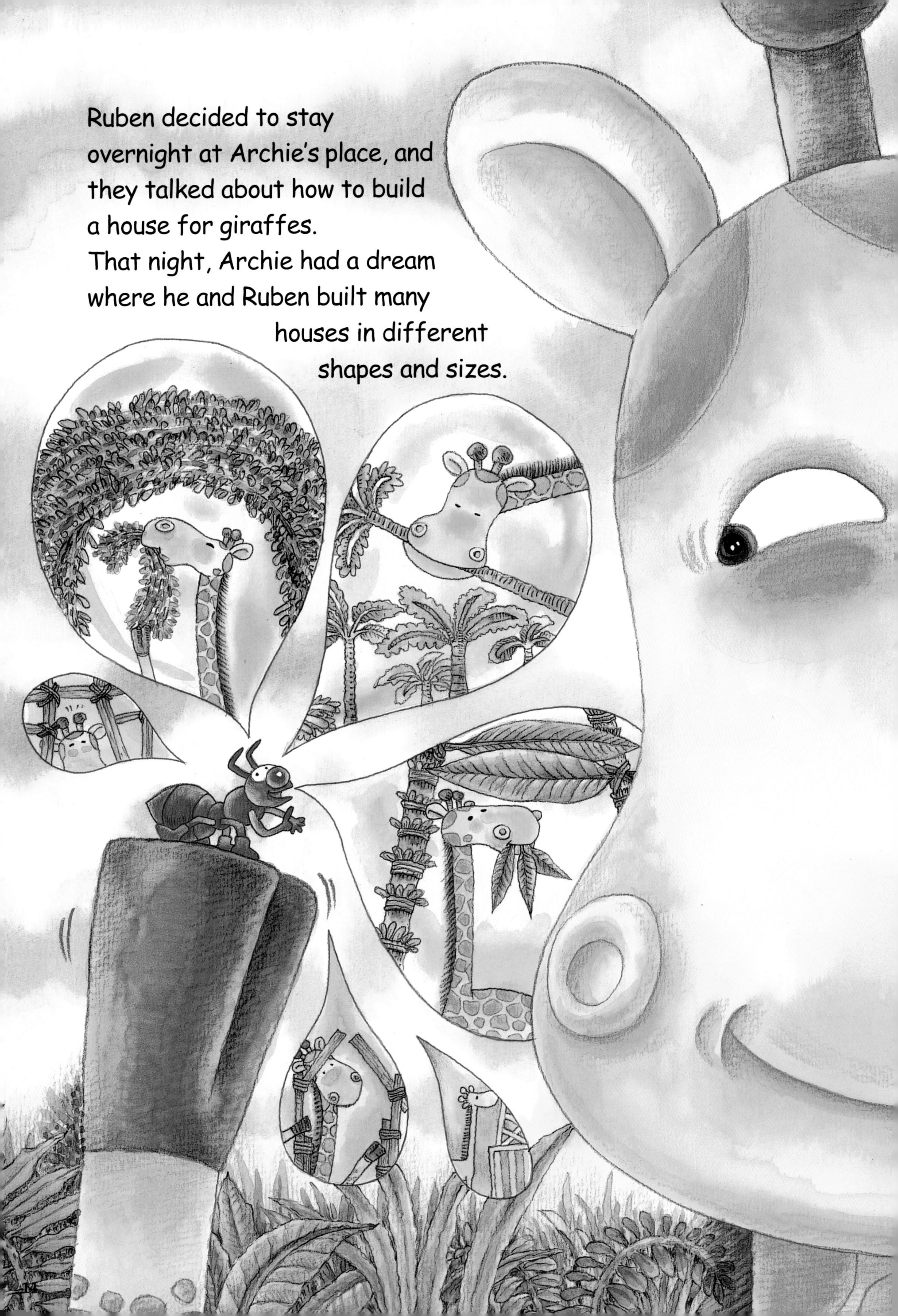

At night the wind started blowing in the field. Ruben was worried, "It looks like a storm is coming!"

Whoo! Whoo! The wind started to blow!
Here comes the storm!
Crack! Thump! The Earth shook!
Here comes an earth quake!
Splish! Splash! Waves crashed!
Here comes a flood!

In the storm, Archie and his big family huddled in a boat made of a Bodhi leaf.

In the darkness, Ruben was worried, and he kept looking around for Archie and his family.
"I can't see them."
"Got you!"
"All right!"

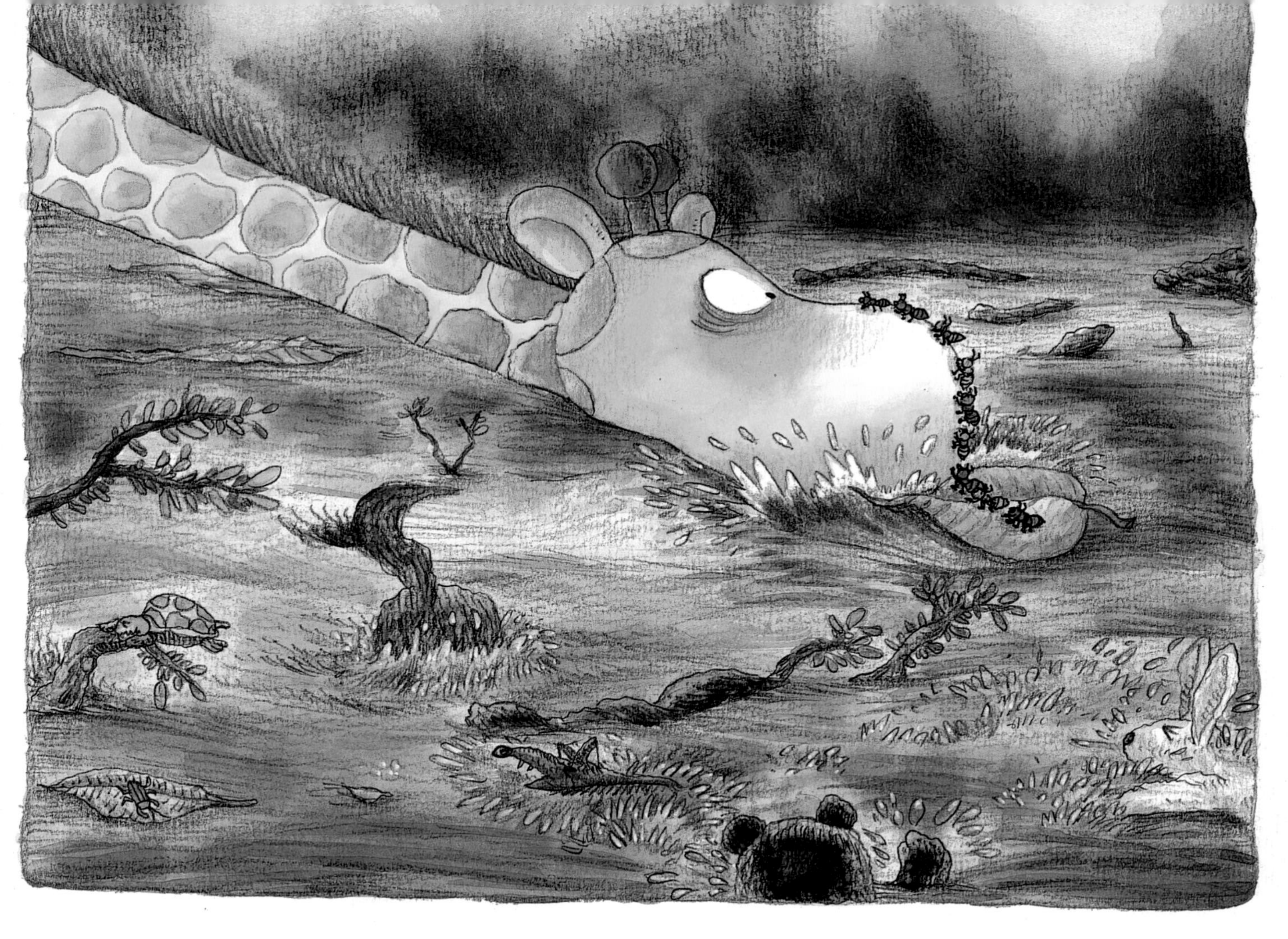

Ruben let Archie's whole family hide in his ear.
Brave Ruben, like a big ship sailing in dangerous water, was loaded with refugees from the storm.

Archie was sad and cried, “My home is gone and so are all my treasures.”

After the storm, everyone got together and looked at the field. It used to be their home, but now only a Bodhi tree was left. Ruben tried to cheer up everyone who once lived there, "As long as you work together, you'll have a wonderful new home! Wherever there is love, there is hope. We'll be as strong as the Bodhi tree."

Archie was still upset, "Even...even the wax apple trees are gone."

Ruben tried to comfort him, "Archie, don't be sad! Look at me! I don't have a house, but wherever I go it's my home."

"You aren't me," Archie said plaintively, wiping away tears. "You're tall and strong! You can live anywhere, but I can't. I'm different!"

He added, "Do you know how much I envy you?"

"One little breath from you and I'd be gone!"

Archie went on, "One of your steps takes me hours to catch up to."

Archie pouted, "You'll never understand. There's no use talking about it anymore!"

Ruben sighed and thought quietly, "Little Archie, you have no idea how much I also envy you."
Not knowing what to say, Ruben left quietly.

"The new houses are finished!" With cheerful spirits, everyone had helped to rebuild their home.

Archie, who hadn't seen Ruben for a long time, felt sorry and wanted to apologize to him.
"Did my attitude upset him?"
"Or maybe he's just made some new friends and doesn't like me anymore!"
"Did I say something wrong?"

Upon the completion of their new home, the inhabitants of the Tee-Hee Field decided to throw a thank-you party for everyone who had helped.

Archie didn't know there was a secret......

Shy Ruben wanted Archie to be like he was before, sitting between his rounded horns, laughing freely, singing and falling asleep. There were so many things he wanted to say to Archie.

Ruben hid behind a bush so that Archie couldn't see him. Banging here and banging there, Ruben was practicing drums in secret.
He felt the drums could help him bring out the words he couldn't say to Archie.

It's show time!
A string quartet was performed by Sika Deer, Big Black Bear, Monkey and Raccoon. Little White Elephant, Kangaroo, Koala Bear and Centipede played the bamboo flute, *erhu*, banjo and zither.

The choir was formed by Hippopotamus, the Rabbit brothers, Cloud Leopard, Mikado Pheasant and the Large Tree Frog sisters.

The Woodpecker friends, Turtle, Rattlesnake, the Bee family and the Cricket kids played percussion.

Archie's relatives and the Spider clan worked together to make characters that spelled the words COURAGE and HAPPINESS.

Red Flamingo and White Flamingo did a harvest dance, and Peacock performed Guanyin Bodhisattva's thousand-hands-and-eyes dance.
The Chimpanzee couple did a King Kong dance, while the Barbet flock, Blue Magpie and Garuda did a flying-apsara dance.

Big Crocodile also wanted to do a dance, but everyone agreed it suited him better just to lie there and be the stage.

The secret guest performed the highlight of the show – Ruben's talking tambourines.

It was his moment.
Nobody made a sound.
The beats of the drum flowed
through the quiet field!

Ruben was speaking to Archie with his drum.
What did he want to say?
Maybe we can guess together!
Will our answers be the same or not the same?

## Blessing card

Do you know anyone that needs to be cheered up? Write down your blessing in the heart-shaped space.

## Gratitude card

Do you want to thank anyone? Write down your words in the heart-shaped space.

## Huimin Bhikshu

President, Dharma Drum Buddhist College (DDBC), Doctor of Letters, Tokyo University

### The Paradox and Realization of "To Be the Same or Not To Be the Same"

Let's think together:
What do Ruben the Giraffe and Archie the Ant have in common? And what makes them different?
In the world that Ruben looks down on from the clouds and that Archie looks up at from the ground, can you find things that are the same and things that are not the same?
How do we look at the facts that we are the same and/or not the same as others?
Can the Earth, Ocean, Fire and Wind, and insignificant humans be friends like Ruben and Archie?
Do the Earth, Ocean, Fire and Wind, and insignificant humans fight like Ruben and Archie?
How do the Earth, Ocean, Fire and Wind, and insignificant humans form long-lasting friendships?
Why doesn't Ruben's good intention to comfort Archie get a positive response?
Why does Archie envy Ruben? And why does Ruben envy Archie?
What problems will be caused by their envy of each other?
How can Ruben and Archie become friends again?
What can shy Ruben do to express what's on his mind?
In the group performances, we can find similarities and differences in the combinations of animals. What are they?
We can bring these ideas, as well as the perspective of "being the same or not being the same" to our discussions with children about interpersonal relationships, conflicts, the integration of races and other social issues. Perhaps we need to have a mentality of tolerance and appreciation so that we can face the world of "difference in sameness" and "sameness in difference" with the right attitude and realize the truth that there is no difference and no sameness.

## Shyryan Cheng

Psychologist

This is a heart-warming and imaginative picture book for children. The lively and animated content can bring out compassion and loving-kindness in children, and therefore helps to plant seeds of healthy relationships and social awareness. From the point of view of literature, the book conveys an air of purity and creativity. The colorful illustrations of the vast world open up new spatial concepts for children.
If children read this book with an adult, they will have a deeper sense of wisdom and joy.

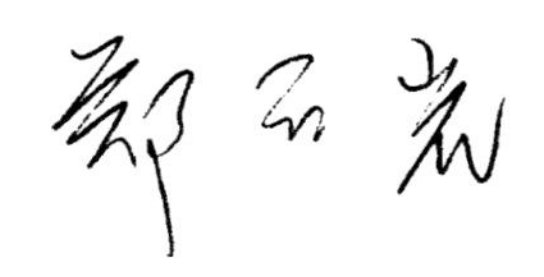

## From the Author

Ruben and Archie 3 is dedicated to a broadcaster who perished in the tsunami on March 11, 2011 in Japan. She stayed at her post until the last moment, when the waves took her life. This book is also written for tsunami victims everywhere.
I frequently had to go through the agony of missing my loved ones when they left the world willingly or unwillingly. I therefore sympathize with all parting in life.
The flow of energy in our lives and reincarnation come from our own choices. We may choose to change from one path to another, or just float around without taking any path. Everything is affected by our will. It is important, therefore, that we know how to keep our mind balanced in good and bad situations, so that our energy stays positive.
I have suffered through attachment to love and the pain caused by it. Through Dharma, I have learned that compassion exists wherever there is love, as does hope. Because of compassion, we can accept each other's differences.
It is difficult to be born as a human being. Imagination is the most precious gift given to us as humans. It is a pair of wings that lets us fly out of windows to freedom. This is an important theme conveyed in this book.
We wish to comfort anyone who's ever suffered and hope that every grownup and child can be inspired by this book.

*Ju-Yarn Tsai*

## From the illustrator

During the nine months it took to illustrate this book, emotional ups and downs were constant. Something unexpected also happened. My right arm was critically injured. The pain started from my shoulder and went down to my fingers. It was difficult to raise and move my hand. In order not to delay publication, I had to endure the pain and get the book finished.
Many thanks to all the people that helped to bring about the publication of this book. We hope that everyone can enjoy this story about the friendship between Big Ruben and Little Archie.

*Chih-Ming Huang*